THE GREAT CAKE DISASTER

Other Bin Weevils books to collect:

Bin Weevils: The Official Guide

Bin Weevils Puzzle Book

Bin Weevils Joke Book

Bin Weevils: Tink and Clott's Search-and-Find Adventure

Bin Weevils Doodle Storybook: Lab's Critter Contraption

Bin Weevils Sticker Activity Book

Bin Weevils Choose Your Own Path 2:
The Mysterious Silence of Scribbles

BACKWARDS BONUS!

Hold this page up to a mirror to reveal a secret code,
then enter it into the Mystery Code Machine
at Lab's Lab to unlock an exclusive nest item!

Ọ4ᗅᎶ⅃8Ɛ3Ɔ∂ƲᎮ⅁

CHOOSE YOUR OWN PATH

BIN Weevils .COM

THE GREAT CAKE DISASTER

Written by Mandy Archer

MACMILLAN CHILDREN'S BOOKS

First published 2012 by Macmillan Children's Books
a division of Macmillan Publishers Limited
20 New Wharf Road, London N1 9RR
Basingstoke and Oxford
Associated companies throughout the world
www.panmacmillan.com

ISBN 978-1-4472-0531-9

1 3 5 7 9 8 6 4 2

A CIP catalogue record for this book is available from
the British Library.

Printed and bound by CPI Group (UK) Ltd, Croydon CR0 4YY

It's another weevily day in the Binscape!

Today your pals Tink and Clott have come over to admire your Bin Nest's shelftastic new trophy room. You've cleaned out most of your Mulch stash buying fancy pedestals and accessories to kit it out, but the spending spree was totally worth it. Now the three of you are chillaxing indoors, hoping for a visit from the Nest Inspector.

'When the Inspector spots how awesome your nest is looking, you're bound to earn yourself a gold Bin Nest Trophy!' grins Tink. 'It can take pride of place in your new room!' he adds, pointing up to your weevily wall furniture.

You can't help but cheer when your mailbox starts to rattle and shake – it's got to be a message from the Nest Inspector!

You open the mailbox and grab the envelope, your antennae trembling with excitement. But instead of finding a note from the Nest Inspector, you're surprised to read a buddy message from Slum, Tum's unglamorous assistant! The message is sludge-splattered and to the point:

DESPERATELY NEED YOUR HELP – EMERGENCY AT TUM'S DINER! REPORT IN TO SECRET WEEVIL SERVICE AT ONCE. AM STICKING MY HEAD IN THE SMELLY JELLY UNTIL THINGS CALM DOWN. SLUM

'We gotta go!' you cry, scrambling out of the trophy room. Something must be very wrong for slow-witted Slum to write for help – Tum's Diner is the happiest, healthiest restaurant in the Binscape! Tink and Clott don't hesitate for a second: helping Bin Weevils in trouble is right at the heart of the Bin Weevil code!

You lean on the portrait of Secret Agent Clott that

hangs so innocently in your nest's entrance hall. Suddenly the portrait slides away to reveal a locked safe. Within seconds that safe is creaking open, revealing an access route to Castle Gam, HQ of the Secret Weevil Service! You report to the mission room at once, desperate to hear the brief for this sudden and intriguing new assignment.

Inside the mission room, Gam is waiting for you. As everybody in the Bin knows, the chief of the SWS is the oldest Bin Weevil around and one of the smartest, too. He's a distinguished soldier who's been operational since the first Bin Day. No one knows exactly how old he is – even he isn't sure!

'Come in, Agents,' he mutters, swivelling round in his chair.

You gulp down a gasp of surprise. The old war vet is looking tired and more ancient than ever – even his wrinkles have got wrinkles! You also notice that the soldier has wedged a handful of slime into each ear.

'I need to tell you about a brand new mission,' sighs Gam. 'I'm sure you know that my birthday is coming up.'

You and Tink roll your eyes. Doh! How could you have forgotten? Gam's birthday is only twenty-four hours away – a massive occasion that's even been declared a Bin bank holiday!

Clott shifts awkwardly on his stool as he remembers that he still hasn't bought Gam a present! You make a mental note to pick up something from the Shopping Mall, then ask the chief to tell you more.

Gam admits that while birthdays are usually a great excuse to strut his stuff with the young 'uns at Club Fling, this year he has something different in mind. He's booked restaurant owners and caterers extraordinaire Tum and Figg to put on a huge birthday feast for all his friends. The venue is Slam's Party Box and it's gonna be mega!

You dribble at the very thought – Tum's Diner and Figg's Cafe are the best eateries in the Bin! Sadly however, things haven't gone to plan. Tum and Figg got so over-competitive over the baking of the birthday cake, the pair have fallen out big-style! Refusing to work together, both ladies have vowed to make their own cake for Gam, each one bigger and better than the other's.

You and your fellow agent Tink nod your heads in sympathy, but Clott simply shrugs his shoulders. 'Would it really be a problem if you have two cakes?' he asks, before winking. 'I could always help you eat 'em!'

'Not only are Tum and Figg fighting,' frowns Gam, 'they are also sabotaging each other's plans. Figg has written a slanderous letter about Tum and sent it off to *Weevil Weekly* magazine. Tum replied by marching to the Haggle Hut loaded up with all her unwanted kitchen equipment. After striking a deal with Nab, she used the extra Mulch to buy up all the birthday candles in the Bin just so Figg couldn't get her hands on them. Now her assistant Slum is distraught without his tools, while Figg was last seen hurling four plates at a time at any Bin Weevil silly enough to suggest that Tum might win the battle of the birthday cakes.'

Gam gestures to his plugged-up ears, a last defence against the barrage of complaints he's had to listen to from the competitive cooks.

'*Now* I get it,' says Clott, nodding sheepishly.

Gam points a bony finger at you.

'The mission is simple,' he says seriously. 'You, Tink

3

and Clott have to get the warring Bin Weevils to make up and bake up, or you'll need to rustle up the birthday cake yourselves!'

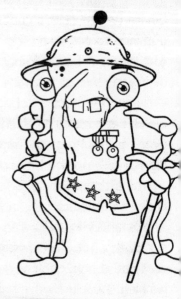

You gulp – you need to sort out this feud, fast! As you leave Gam gives you a pot of chocolate sludge and a beaker full of crushed beetle meringue to put in your backpack. He agrees to see you tomorrow – his birthday!

Now your mission is set, you have some important decisions to make.
Will you start by taking your chances plate-dodging at Figg's Cafe or run to comfort flustered Slum at Tum's Diner?

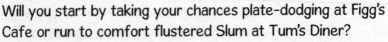

If you decide to visit Figg's Cafe, go to page 77.
If you think it's better to help out Slum, go to page 21.

'Share what?' asks a curious voice.

You pass Lucky to your friends, then slowly turn round to face Figg! The cafe owner waves hello, then tries to peer over your shoulder to find out what you're looking at.

'N-nothing!' you say brightly, thinking on your feet. 'But we've been meaning to come and see you. It's this row about Gam's birthday cake. That letter you wrote to *Weevil Weekly* didn't really go down too well at Tum's Diner . . .'

You stop jabbering. Figg isn't even listening! Instead she has scooped Lucky up and is cooing affectionately in his ear. The little Bin Pet wriggles closer.

'What a cutie!' she squeals. 'I love him, I love him!'

'That's Lucky,' you explain. 'We're giving him to Gam for his birthday.'

Figg gets to her feet, snuggling the Bin Pet in her pinny. 'You can't do that! Gam's far too old. He'll never be able to give him the exercise he needs.'

'What else do we do with him?' asks Tink.

'I would offer to have the adorable little mite,' Figg sighs to herself. 'But I'm far too busy with this cake and all . . .'

As if on cue, the pet stretches its arms out for a little Binny hug. Figg is in love.

The arrangements don't take a trice to sort out. Now she's found Lucky, Figg is happy to let Tum bake to her heart's content! She skips back to her nest, promising to bring Lucky to Gam's party the next day.

Feud forgotten. Re-sult!!!

The End

5

'Don't cry, Tum,' you soothe, trying to resist the urge to dip your finger in all that yummy melted mud. 'I'll think of something.'

'You haven't got a clue, have you?' she wails. 'Everything's ruined! I knew my quadruple sludge topping was too good to be true!'

Tink and Clott take turns passing hankies to the heartbroken chef while you do some serious thinking. You pace up and down the Party Box at least a dozen times. Tum's tears and the mess on the floor add up to a recipe for disaster, but maybe it's the breakthrough you've been searching for all along!

You scan the venue for Fink. In the corner Fling is practising a new dance routine ready for the party – that Bin Weevil can really move! The rest of the place appears empty, until you spot a very familiar navy blue helmet sticking out from behind a pillar.

'Fink!' you whisper. 'Get over here!'

Before you know it Fink has launched himself into a dramatic forward roll across the dance floor, landing at your feet in a panting heap.

'Reporting in for duty,' he says dramatically.

You roll your eyes. He really could have just walked.

'I've got an important job for you,' you say. 'Go and get Figg!'

What happens when Figg meets Tum?
Turn to page 41 where the jaw-dropping
answer is waiting!

'I like your thinking, Tink,' you say weakly, 'but we need to keep going. You and Clott don't exactly have a high success rate when it comes to hatching plans.'

Tink sighs forlornly.

'Next time,' you insist.

The three of you stop to take in the awesome sight ahead. Tink's Tree fills the horizon, its heavy branches laden with pink blossom and icky, sticky fruit. If you could just get the tree to produce a shiny new seed, Tum would be totally impressed! You're sure it will convince her that when it comes to birthday bashes, two cooks are better than one.

Tink and Clott run ahead and start clambering up the purple Step Mushrooms sprouted around the roots of the tree.

'Whoa!' you bellow. 'We've go to work together, remember?'

If Tink's Tree is going to produce an ultra-cool seed, you know you're going to have to feed it. You ask Tink and Clott to climb higher and higher up the branches, until they reach a gloopy yellow fly nest. You quickly run to the nearest Scent Flower, allowing it to squelch you in its pongy fog.

'Now jump on the nest!' you cry.

Tink and Clott jump with all their might. A flock of flies buzz out of the nest, flying off in search of something sweet. Your eau-de-Scent Flower is perfect – within moments, you are surrounded by the biggest bug swarm ever! You stagger towards the tree's knotty roots. Tink and Clott cheer loudly when a tongue curls out of the nearest one and sucks the flies up! Now the tree is fed, all you've got do is wait . . .

. . . and wait . . .

. . . and wait and w-a-i-t.

'Wake up, weev!'

You give a wide yawn, then flinch in surprise. How did you manage to fall asleep on the job?

'Look!' cries Tink, pointing to the tree. The ancient plant is laden down with more ripe fruit than you've ever seen in all your time in the Bin!

'I can see a shiny new seed up there. It's just about to drop!' squeals Clott.

And there it is. A very special acorn with a pair of golden wings.

Word travels fast in the Binscape. Dozens of Bin Tycoons rush up to the Tree, trying to get their greedy paws on your seed!

'Spread out!' you cry, jostling to get a place underneath the right branches. 'There she goes!'

You move left a bit, right a bit and then dive . . .

'Gotcha!'

Tink and Clott cheer as you catch the seed in one hand! The three of you stop to admire the prize. This little seed proves just what Bin Weevils can do with a bit of teamwork!

> Now you've got the seed, what are you going to do with it? If you decide to stay and grow another one, go to page 52.
> If you decide to take it back to Tum's Diner, go to page 86.

Clott wheels the Scent Flower down the grubby lane that leads to Flum's Fountain. Every few metres, the bloom spritzes you with its floral smell. Passing Bin Weevils stop to sniff and admire the fine plant. You even get offered a wad of Mulch for it by an envious Bin Tycoon!

'Stop a second, Clott!' you whisper. 'We've got something very special here.'

Tink nods, standing back to admire the Scent Flower's ruby petals and bold-striped trumpet. 'Do you know who'd really like this?' he says.

You and Clott both give the same reply.

'Gam.'

Tink claps his hands. 'Yes! Something this rare would make the perfect birthday present. Can we give it to him? Can we? CAN WE?!'

You decide to take a quick vote. The result totals up to three resounding 'yes's!

'Every time he sniffs it, he'll think of us,' you beam.

The three of you push on for Castle Gam. It's only when you're about to walk into the SWS headquarters that you remember that you haven't e-x-a-c-t-l-y* solved the birthday cake mission, but hey, you're certain that this super-duper pressie will win the old fella round.

Fingers crossed!

The End

*Or at all, in fact!

Before you know it you are all standing in the mud outside Tum's Diner. Clott stares purposefully at the sliding doors.

'What are we going to do now?' you ask, impressed by your pal's bravado.

Clott takes one look at the restaurant sign and snorts.

'Well we're not going in there!' he guffaws, dragging you across the dirt. 'We're going in *there*!'

He leads you and Tink towards the bright lights of Rum's Airport.

'We're catching the first flight to Mulch Island,' says Clott proudly. 'It's a dream destination!'

Clott steers you both through the airport check-in. Soon you are boarding a bumpy Weevil Air flight to the far-off holiday isle. Excited Bin Weevils in the seats next to you chatter about Mulch Island's desert sands, warm seas and exotic ruins.

When you arrive, you discover that Mulch Island is sunny, sandy and crawling with exotic wildlife – everything you want from a holiday and more! After you've bagged yourselves a frosty snack from the Ice Cream Machine, you sit down to soak up the sun.

'This is the life!' decides Tink, stretching out underneath an orange parasol.

Clott replies with a satisfied nod. For a long time the three of you sit in silence listening to the waves lap up the beach.

Soon you can't stand it any longer.

'Sorry, Clott,' you say, 'but what are we doing here? How is this going to solve the impending birthday cake catastrophe?'

Tink and Clott look baffled.

'It's not!' they both say at once. Rather than crack the cake feud, the Bin Boys explain their ingenious new plan to lie low until all the trouble is over.

'Tum and Figg are hopping mad about Gam's birthday,' says Clott. 'We'll never win 'em round! Now we can afford to stay out of the way until all the fuss has died down.'

'But . . . ! B–but,' you splutter.

Tink shoves another chocolate ice cream into your mitt. You can't resist giving it a lick. De-lish-uss! You've failed in your mission, but at least you're on track to bag a mighty fine sun tan!

The End

11

'Of all the places in the Bin . . .' splutters Clott, peeking out of the Mystery Portal. 'Can we go back?'

'Nope,' you reply, squinting beneath the fluorescent lights of Tum's Diner!

You, Tink and Clott crawl through the crowded restaurant and take a seat at a table in the corner. You spot Slum standing near the jukebox, wiping his nose with the back of his hand. A thirsty Bin Weevil asks him for a shake, but he sends them away. The poor kitchen-hand is lost without his liquidizer!

'Slum's in a right state,' groans Tink. 'Shall I go and cheer him up with one of my jokes?'

You shake your head. There's no time for that now. You need to get to Tum and talk her round.

'When I say three, I want you to follow me into the kitchen,' you whisper, keeping your head low. 'Three!'

One by one you make a dash for it. Irritated customers grumble loudly as you dive past them. There's a loud gasp when Clott's elbow knocks a Double Bin Burger off a table, but you catch it just in the nick of time. You pop the snack back, smile and hand a serviette to the confused Bin Weevil about to eat his tea.

Within seconds you're standing outside the doorway to Tum's private domain.

'Cover me, Agents,' you say bravely. 'I'm going in!'

You push your way through the doorway and storm across the tiles, yelling like a wild Bin Weevil.

Tum yells back. 'Aaagggggghhhh!'

After the yelling stops, you and Tum stare at each other in stunned silence. The chef speaks first.

'What the stink are you doing in my kitchen?' she asks.

You decide to give it to her straight.

'We've been sent by the SWS to stop this ridiculous feud with Figg,' you announce boldly. 'If you don't call a truce I won't be held responsible for my actions.'

Tum grabs a wooden spoon, barring the way to the giant Chocolate Sludge Cake standing on the table behind her.

'What have you got in mind?' she demands. 'Do your worst!'

You turn to ask Tink and Clott for back-up, but they've already darted out of the room. Now Tum is looking fierce, armed and bigger than you. You need to think on your feet. Or even using your brain would do.

'I could wreak havoc in here,' you reply casually, 'but before I do, would you care for a bite of Dirt Doughnut? They're absolutely de-lish!'

You stick your hand in your pocket and pull out one of Figg's treats. Tum's eyes blaze with fury, but then she catches a sniff of the sugar grit topping. The recipe has been a closely guarded secret of the Rigg family for years. Tum has tried making doughnuts before, but her creations don't even come close.

Tum looks up and down to make sure no one else is looking. You've whetted her culinary interest! The temptation to try her rival's speciality is too much to resist.

'Give it here,' she replies, sinking her teeth into the delectable dough. 'Mmmmm! So this is what Figg is making for Gam's birthday?'

'That's right,' you confirm, 'but do you know what? I think you should *let* her make them. A Dirt Doughnut birthday cake is very tasty and all that, but Gam won't like it.'

Tum's eyes grow wide. She leans in a little closer.

'Won't he?'

You shake your head, reminding the competitive cook how many teeth the old soldier has. He won't be able to chew through half a doughnut without losing his gnashers, let alone a whole stack! You cleverly suggest that she focuses instead on making a giant, show-stopping dessert – Tum's Jelly!

Tum's eyes light up.

'My jelly is very popular,' she agrees. 'Even better than my Chocolate Sludge Cake!'

'We'll help eat up that Sludge Cake,' you say kindly, pointing to the sponge in the corner. 'You focus on being the queen of the desserts!'

Tum sweeps out of the kitchen in search of her biggest jelly mould. A bit of quick thinking has ended the battle of the birthday cakes and earned enough Chocolate Sludge Cake to keep you, Tink and Clott fed for weeks!

The End

'Scribbles!' you plead. 'Tum and Figg will go potty when they read that story. It'll ruin Gam's birthday!'

The editor stops typing to think things over. It's a tricky decision. He's been looking forward to the party as much as the next Bin Weevil and he'd hate to see Gam's day spoilt.

'Nope!' he finally decides. 'It's against my journalistic principles. I can't ignore the facts!'

'So does that mean you're not going to run it?' asks Tink hopefully.

'No, it means I *am* going to run it!' he replies. 'It's my job to keep the Binscape informed. And besides, I haven't got anything else for the headline story.'

It's a long shot, but you decide to seize your chance.

'I've got a suggestion,' you stammer. 'How about a different angle?'

'Like what?'

'Well . . .' you begin, desperately trying to buy time. 'I mean, erm, well! What's the word on the street? A few hard-hitting interviews could bring this story to life. Who knows, we might even dig up some exciting new info on the "Warring Bin Weevils"!'

You've got the editor interested!

'I'll hold the press for half an hour,' he agrees. 'Get me the dirt!'

Where will you head? If you decide to make a
Bin-line for Flum's Fountain, go to page 40.
If you decide to check out what the crowds at
Tycoon Plaza are saying, go to page 23.

You give the acorn a little polish with the back of your hand, then stride through the sliding doors of Tum's Diner. It's time to see if your hard work has paid off! Tink pops a disk on the jukebox, while Clott knocks gently on the kitchen door.

'Not now!' shouts Tum's voice.

You gulp. This is going to be harder than you'd first thought.

'We just want to have a chat,' you plead, pushing the door ajar.

'Get Slum to take your order,' blusters Tum. 'I'm busy!'

Slum lands at your feet in a heap, then the door is slammed shut again.

'D-d-don't go in there!' he warns. 'She's having problems with her Chocolate Sludge Cake. It's starting to melt.'

Tink and Clott don't need any more persuading.

'Righto, champ,' says Tink, giving a farewell salute.

'Is that the time?' asks Clott. 'We'll be off then . . .'

'Hold on one roly-mo!' you cry. 'Don't be maggots! It's time to show the whole Bin why Gam sent us on this mission. We're going in!'

You hand the acorn to Slum, then push your way into Tum's kitchen. The harassed chef is standing on a stepladder, trying to pipe melted mud on to her cake. Piles of birthday candles are stacked up on every spare surface, giving the air a sticky, waxy smell. Giant globules of sludgy sponge drip over the worktop and on to the grungy floor.

'Now listen here, Tum!' you shout. 'You need to stop this silliness with Figg! We've gone to a lot of trouble to get hold of a seed from Tink's Tree just to show you how important teamwork is. You can't just take over Gam's birthday feast. You're not the only cook in the Bin, you know . . .'

You catch the look on Tum's chocolate-splattered face and trail off the lecture.

'Don't worry,' she gulps. 'My cake hasn't worked out. Figg can cook whatever she likes!'

Tum begins to sob. You shift awkwardly from left to right as big, salty tears fall on to her bungled baking. You can't help but feel a little bit sorry for her.

'There, there,' you say. 'What went wrong?'

'My cake came out a treat,' Tum sighs, 'but when I decided to test run the hundred candles on top, the sponge started to melt! I took them all off, but it's too late. Look at it. I mean, *look*!'

It is indeed a miserable sight. What a waste of good sludge!

You run your finger along the edge of the table and take a lick. Yum! Up till now, Figg's Dirt Doughnuts have always been your snack of choice, but Tum's sponge has got the wow factor in droves.

'That's it!' you suddenly cry, scrabbling to find the diner's comedy Bin Burger telephone. 'What this cake needs is a ring of Dirt Doughnuts all around the edge.'

Tink whoops with delight, while Clott makes a dash for the restaurant.

'That would stop it spilling on to the floor!' he marvels. 'Inspired!'

You have to admit it is a truly genius idea. If Figg can supply the doughnuts, the pair could create a cake par excellence!

Tum stops sobbing.

'Do you think she'd agree to a joint collaboration?' she asks sheepishly. 'We did have such a terrible spat.'

'Already has!' grins Clott, bursting back into the kitchen. 'Dialled her up meself!'

It takes several minutes for the backslapping and cheering to calm down.

'It's going to be super!' sings Tum. 'I think we'd better leave the candles off though, don't you?'

'I have a better idea for a centrepiece,' you grin.

You place the seed from Tink's Tree in pride of place at the top of Tum's cake. The verdict? Bin Birthday brilliant!

The End

You boldly dive behind the mushroom and tackle the Bin Weevil round the legs. The flustered stranger tumbles to the ground with a high-pitched 'Eek!'

'Oh, heck,' gulps Tink. 'It's Figg!'

Figg clambers up to her feet.

'What are you doing here?' she splutters. 'You're supposed to be delivering my Doughnut Tower.'

Clott asks her the same thing. The last time you saw Figg she was working hard in the cafe!

Figg explains that she came to Lab's Lab to earn a few more Mulch, just like you.

'I wanted to buy some extra toppings to sprinkle on my Dirt Doughnut Tower,' she sighs, before admitting that she only got two questions right.

Your eyes start to twinkle. You unzip your rucksack and pull out the beaker full of crushed beetle meringue and the pot of chocolate sludge that Gam gave you at the start of the mission.

'What about using these?' you say.

Figg claps her hands. 'Yes please!'

You agree to dish out the tasty ingredients on one condition – that she makes up the silly fight with Tum!

Figg thinks long and hard. She so wants to refuse, but the tasty snack is just too good to resist! In a rash moment of weakness, she agrees to go round to see Tum straight away.

'Happy days,' winks Tink. 'Let's report back to Castle Gam!'

The End

19

Posh sashays past, her little Bin Pet, Lady Wawa, scuttling behind her. She's the most sophisticated Bin Weevil in town, and so far out of Clott's league it gives you a nosebleed just thinking about it.

'You were saying, Bunty?' you urge, desperate to keep Clott focused on the mission in hand. 'Why do you think Tum and Figg are so keen to make Gam's birthday cake?'

Bunty lowers her voice and steps closer.

'It's all about fame,' she whispers. 'Tum and Figg both want it! The chef that's responsible for Gam's birthday cake is bound to be the talk of the Binscape. Who knows, they might even get to land their own TV show off the back of it! Tum and Figg would both do anything, *anything*, to win a gig like that.'

Bunty has a point. Everyone knows that Figg is a wannabe TV-star. Tum pitches her cookery programme idea, 'Telly Bellies', to any Bin Weevil that will listen.

You, Tink and Clott walk Bunty down to Tycoon Plaza.

'I'd better go to work now,' she grins, disappearing into the super-swanky Tycoon Shop. 'See ya!'

If you decide to do some scouting in the Photo Shop, go to page 27.

If you'd rather take a minute to check on business in Clott's Garden Plots, go to page 50.

You salute Gam and puff out your chest, assuring him that he won't be disappointed in choosing you for this special mission! The old soldier suggests you could use some extra SWS Agent training before you get started, but you laugh in the face of such foolishness. You turn on your heel and sweep out of the mission room, leaving Tink and Clott to pick their jaws up off the floor.

'A-ha!' you cry, grabbing a door handle and yanking with all your might. A grungy mop and a feather duster tumble on to your head. 'The way out must be over . . . here!'

Gam winces, then points to the door next to it with the big 'EXIT' sign at the top. You calmly return the mop and feather duster to the broom cupboard, then proceed to make your way out of the castle.

By the time you are back outside breathing the fresh air of the Binscape, you've already hatched an ingenious plan. You, Tink and Clott need to get yourselves over to Tum's Diner, sharpish! You're convinced that you can persuade Tum to give up the cake feud with Figg. The three of you have consumed more of Tum's Bin Burgers than the rest of her regulars put together – that must make you practically family! All you need to do is put on a pinny and spend half an hour talking the old gal round.

Unfortunately, when you stroll into the diner a little later, you don't exactly get the welcome you expected.

'If Figg sent you,' shrieks Tum, 'tell her we're closed!'

The cook storms back into her kitchen, leaving you standing speechless in front of the jukebox.

'She's stinking crazy!' wails Slum. 'She flipped when she heard that Gam had asked Figg to help make his birthday feast. Tum had already made a giant

21

Chocolate Sludge Cake with extra melted mud, but now she's threatening to throw it in the bin. You gotta help!'

A loud clatter and bang ring out from the kitchen.

'What's she doing now?' asks Tink.

'Counting her stash of birthday candles,' replies Slum. 'If there aren't a hundred I'll be for it!'

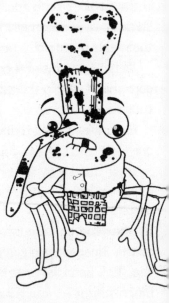

Clott tries to push the door open, but Slum stands in his way.

'Don't go in there,' he warns. 'Tum took my liquidizer to the Haggle Hut when I tried to talk to her. Who knows what she'll do to you!'

Slum pours you a quick shake to slurp while you think things over. How can you talk Tum round? Unless she can be persuaded to buddy up with Figg, Gam's party is in serious jeopardy!

Actions speak louder than words! If you decide to prove to Tum that teamwork is best, go to page 35.
If you decide to visit the Haggle Hut first and buy back Slum's stuff, go to page 87.

'Now what are we going to do?' yelps Tink, following you and Clott out of Flem Manor into the fresh air of the Bin.

'We've got to find ourselves some news that's going to bump Figg and Tum's bust-up off the front page!'

'I've got some news,' pipes up Clott, trying to be helpful. 'Instead of easy-peasy porridge I treated meself to slugs on toast this morning!'

Tink bursts into an enthusiastic round of applause, then gives his pal a big thumbs up. Sometimes you worry about those two.

'Let's head over to Tycoon Island,' you suggest. 'We've only got twenty-three minutes left. Come on!'

You are soon rubbing shoulders with the rich, grubbily rich and downright filthy rich in the Plaza on Tycoon Island. Everyone here is super-swanky and they know it too! You scuttle desperately round Dosh's golden statue, gawping at the shop windows stacked high with super-expensive gear. Clott frowns at you. This place is packed with Bin millionaires, but no one looks like they've got a sensational story to tell.

You wander over to the Photo Shop and peer inside. Snappy, the Bin's photography expert, gives you a friendly wave.

'Er . . . maybe now's not the right time to go shopping for camera gear,' grunts Tink. 'We've only got sixteen minutes left to find the story of the century!'

'I'm not,' you reply. 'Look who Snappy's shooting!'

Inside, standing in a spotlight and loving every second, is Ink. A natural show-off, thesp and all-round arty-farty type, Ink is striking more poses than Snappy can snap. The minute he spots you, Ink calls you in.

'Why hello there!' he beams. 'Just having a new

photo taken to promote my latest poetry book. What brings you here?'

'We're looking for a story for the front cover of *Weevil Weekly*,' you explain. 'Got any ideas?'

Ink's face lights up.

'Do I? Of course!' he cries, making a dash for his quill.

You, Tink and Clott perk up a little as Ink pulls out a huge notebook, dropping it on the table with a heavy thud. He flicks through page after page of scribbled handwriting. Snappy decides to take a break – she's seen Ink's inkings before.

'I'm off for a mucka latte with extra sludge,' she sighs, turning the studio sign round to CLOSED. 'You could be some time.'

'We can't be some time!' you reply. You're already down to thirteen minutes and counting!

'There is so much I want to say in *Weevil Weekly*,' says Ink. 'Where shall we start? We could always pick some highlights from my most famous work, *Poems from the Binscape!*'

You flick through Ink's book, scanning the lines. The pages are littered with poems, odes, sonnets and plays, but where's a sensational news story when you need it? You scan as much as you can and then put the pad down.

'This is all good stuff, but I don't think there's anything there that's good enough for the headline story,' you explain. 'Sorry, Ink.'

'Did someone say "headline story"?' says a voice.

You, Tink, Clott and Ink all spin round to see Hem stick her head round the door. At least you think it's Hem. At the moment all you can see is a mass of yellow carnations fixed to an enormous green hat. The Bin Weevil straightens up her headpiece and strides into the Photo Shop.

'If you're looking for ideas, you'd better talk to me,' she continues, before adding, 'Nice waistcoat, Tink, it's rubbish!'

Tink winks at you. As well as owning the hat shop in Tycoon Plaza, Hem has been trying to get herself a column in *Weevil Weekly* since ... forever! She's spent years bombarding Scribbles with requests to write about her fashion escapades and style ideas. Up to now she's had no luck. You glance at the clock on the wall. Nine minutes to go — maybe it's time to give Hem the big break she needs.

While Hem rattles on about hatty headlines, Ink throws down his quill in protest. 'Now hang on!' he protests. 'I know exactly what to put in the magazine. I'll write a brand new work!'

If you decide to hear Hem out, go to page 57.
If you think that Ink's quill power is the only way to impress Scribbles, go to page 67.

'Ooh, help!' you holler. 'Tum and Figg are two tough cookies. I'll never be able to impress these crowds!'

Fling shimmies up next to you, his gold medallion swinging in all directions.

'Did somebody say something about impressing the crowds?' he asks. 'I'm your main man!'

You swap desperate glances with Tink and Clott. It's got to be worth a try!

You sit Fling down and explain the problems you've had trying to sort out the fight between the restaurant owners. If only you could get them to swallow their pride and put the feud behind them!

Fling grins so hard his veneered teeth nearly blind you.

'Get Tum and Figg here, I'll do the rest,' he promises.

Two hours later, you nervously lead Tum and Figg into the Party Box. Fling is waiting on the dance floor. It is no accident that Tum's favourite tune is spinning on the decks.

'Come on down, girls!' he beams, twirling Figg round so hard she comes to a stop thinking it's a week next Tuesday.

There ought to be shouting. There ought to be plate smashing. But somehow the Bin Weevils are putty in Fling's hand. By the time he's ready to teach them a new birthday dance routine, the chefs are hugging and high-kicking to the cancan. All you, Tink and Clott need to do is slip off to the bar, grab an Awesome Poursome and enjoy the show.

The End

'Follow me, chaps,' you say to Tink and Clott, ducking your head into the Photo Shop. Bunty's scoop on the bickering bakers has just given you an idea.

Snappy is inside, happily swinging back and forth on her photographer's chair. She leaps up the second she sees you, grabbing a digital camera from the counter.

'Hold it right there!' she shouts. 'Say cheese!'

Before you know it, your mugshots have been downloaded and projected on to a screen showing a swirly underwater scene.

'Wow!' says Tink, gawping like a fish. 'It's almost like being there!'

Snappy nods proudly.

'I've just created a whole new set of backgrounds that you can put any portrait on,' she explains. She flicks her remote and suddenly you and your pals are flashed up again – this time standing against the backdrop of Flum's Fountain. Another flick and it's Tink's Tree. Another one and you're floating in outer space!

'Bin Weevils on the Moon,' gushes Clott. 'What a totally kew-ell idea!'

Snappy is in her element, thrilled to have found some photo-enthusiasts to talk to. She explains how she can use the computer to add in all sorts of extra props.

'I've got a picture challenge for you, Snappy,' you smile mysteriously.

Snappy's little blue face flushes pink with excitement. You go on.

'I want to create a special picture for Gam's birthday,' you explain, 'starring Tum, Figg and their cake creations! The problem is, I don't think we can get the cooks into the same room before the big day.'

Snappy isn't fazed in the slightest. She flicks on her photo-processing machine and starts scrolling through all manner of fabulous frames.

'If you can get me pictures of Tum and Figg, I'll put something together that will look amazing on Gam's mantelpiece!'

The challenge is on. Snappy lends you two cameras and sends you out to bag some eye-catching poses. You head out to take a photo of Figg and her stack of Dirt Doughnuts, dispatching Tink and Clott to snap Tum with her Chocolate Sludge Cake. You put yourselves under strict instructions not to let the cooks know what you're up to. It's not lying – it's just being creative with the truth! An hour or so later, you all skid back through the Photo Shop door. Snappy gets to work.

The results are spectacular. Snappy presents you with a gold-framed portrait showing Tum and Figg smiling in front of their mouth-watering cakes.

'It looks like they're standing in the same kitchen,' marvels Tink.

'Let's send it in to *Weevil Weekly*,' you suggest. 'There is just time to make the evening edition! When the chefs see that they're the stars of the headline story, they'll drop this fight like a hot potato!'

Tink and Clott are über-impressed. Not only have you sorted out the fiercest cake feud in Bin history, you've also found the ideal birthday present for Gam.

'Well done, Bin Weevils,' grins Snappy. 'See you at the party!'

The End

'Nah,' you decide. 'Figg will be furious if she hears we've taken a detour. We're going to have to get there under our own steam.'

'I'll push,' offers Tink. 'You can pull and Clott can steer.'

'Top idea!' grins Clott, guiding the trolley around a mound of potato peelings. 'Let's go!'

By the time you arrive at the Party Box, your Dirt Doughnuts are looking worse for wear. You've still got a cool hundred, but they've picked up some extra dents, dust splats and fly droppings during the journey. You whistle breezily and push the Tower across the dance floor, hoping the lights are dim enough for no one to notice.

'Hello, Bin Weevils!'

Dosh has turned up to oversee the last few preparations. Trust the Bin millionaire to muscle in on the party of the century! The Tycoon is filling swanky goodie bags with loot for the VIP guests.

'A hundred of my . . . er, Gam's . . . special friends will be getting one of these,' he announces smugly. 'There's my new "Eau de Bog" fragrance, a party hat and a 1,000-Mulch note!'

If you want to push on and deliver Figg's cake, go to page 54.

If you're in the mood to stay and talk goodie bags with Dosh, go to page 90.

Fink drums his finger along the edge of the trolley, then blows his whistle as hard as he can. You jump at the noise.

'Well?' he bellows impatiently. 'I can't help you if you don't tell me what's going on!'

You shoot an apologetic look at Tink, then tell Fink everything. When you're clutching at straws, you've got to explore every option in the Binscape! Fink scribbles down the details, ooh-ing at Tum's candle mischief then aah-ing at Figg's strong letter to *Weevil Weekly*.

'What a fine old turn-up!' he concludes, blowing through his teeth.

'Well?' you demand. 'What do you think we should do?'

Fink explains that he needs more time to sieve through the evidence. He decides to go 'undercover' for a while. While you wheel the trolley towards the Party Box entrance, Fink trails a few metres behind you, leaping out of sight whenever another Bin Weevil passes by.

Before long, the four of you arrive at the venue for Gam's birthday. Slam's Party Box may not look much from the outside, but the inside is a revelation! Streamers and balloons trail from the ceilings, while the dance floor twinkles temptingly in the disco lights. And there, in the middle of all the decorations is Tum, crying into her apron.

'What's up?' you ask, taking care to stand in front of Figg's Doughnut Tower.

Tum points to a squelchy brown heap on the floor.

'Slum dropped my Chocolate Sludge Cake,' she sobs. 'Look at it now!'

You, Tink and Clott gasp. Tum's cake is ruined! The beautiful muddy sponge has been reduced to a sticky goo-splattered mess. Slum is nowhere to be seen,

31

but you imagine the poor kitchen-hand is probably beating himself with a wooden spoon at this very second.

Tum turns to you with a feeble look of hope in her eyes. 'Can you help me?' she sniffs. 'I don't know what to do.'

If you decide to ask Fink to run and fetch Figg,
    go to page 6.
If you think it would be cleverer to find Slum first,
    go to page 53

'I give up!' yells Tink, bumping down the Step
on his bottom. Clott crashes after him, groaning
bounce.

'Take a break, chaps,' you sigh.

You've been here for hours, but Tink's Tree is refusing
to give up any more seeds. They must be rare for a reason!
The three of you head into the tree's hollow trunk to cheer
yourselves up with a quick game of Konnect Mulch.

'What are we gonna do?' asks Clott, beating you for the
fifth time in as many minutes.

'Let's go back to my nest,' you reply. 'We'll have to think of
something else.'

BOIINNKKK!!!!

That's when it hits you. Literally!

As you walk back outside a golden acorn drops down from
Tink's Tree and lands on your head. Bin Weevils push and
shove each other to get a peek at the prize.

'Two seeds!' bellows one jealous Bin Tycoon. 'It really is
your lucky day!'

'Too righty!' you beam.

You link arms with Tink and Clott, then make your
way back. Once you present the ultra-rare seeds to Tum
and Figg, they're bound to forget their fight! Even if the
teamwork angle doesn't have the pair eating out the palm of
your hand, you've bagged yourselves the ultimate bargaining
tool. Two seeds for one big, beautiful birthday cake makes
for a brilliant deal all round. Well done you!

The End

33

and Tink follow Clott all the way to the golden columns of Rigg's Movie Multiplex. It's an impressive sight.

'Oi!'

You reel round to see Rigg himself holding a walkie-talkie to his ear. The builder doesn't look best pleased – he hasn't caught up with Tink and Clott since the day he sacked them for gross incompetence on a building site.

'What are you doing here?' he roars. 'I'm waiting to meet an important new client.'

'That would be me,' Clott beams. 'Ta-daa!'

Rigg's face clouds over, but when Clott hands him a wad of Mulch he decides not to storm away. Clott commissions Rigg to build a very special new structure at Slam's Party Box – a luxury, two-tiered display platform designed to give Tum and Figg's cakes the red carpet treatment.

'We need it in twenty-four hours,' adds Clott. 'OK?'

'My building will be the talk of the Bin!' he promises, scuttling off to find some workers to order about.

'Don't forget,' adds Tink, 'the cakes must have equal billing!'

You can't resist giving Clott a slap on the back. If the display stand is flash enough, Tum and Figg are bound to accept sharing the spotlight. You're pretty certain this mission is solved!

Tink counts the Mulch left under his mate's hat.

'Four hundred and seventy-three,' he announces. 'Just enough to buy back Slum's kitchen stuff . . .'

'. . . and pay for three celebration Bin Scones!' you add.

The End

'Where are we going?' asks Clott, taking off his top hat and rubbing his head. 'We've been walking for ages!'

Poor Tink is already on all sixes, crawling along on his knees.

'Yeah,' he agrees, 'we must have been struggling along like this for at least . . . five minutes.'

'We're going to Tink's Tree,' you announce, pointing to the magical branches twinkling the distance. You know that Tink's Tree is famous for bearing ultra-rare seeds, but only if Bin Weevils work together in teams to keep it well fed. 'If we can get the tree to bear fruit, we just might . . . Tink? Clott?'

You roll your eyes and wait for the sweaty pair to get up off the floor and catch their breath. If only Gong was joining you on this mission instead of the Boys from the Bin! With the medal-mad Bin Weevil on your side, you would have got to Tink's Tree in no time!

'Why are we going there?' mutters Clott. 'Shouldn't we be trying to sort out Gam's birthday cake?'

You stifle a groan, then remind your friends that you are trying to prove a very important point.

'We need to show Tum that teamwork really does pay off,' you explain. 'When she sees what we can achieve together at the tree, she's bound to forget about all this Figg nonsense and get back to flipping Bin Burgers.'

Tink and Clott think the plan over as you walk past Club Fling and the gleaming outline of the Shopping Mall. There's a very long silence. Too long.

'What now?!' you cry, stopping in your tracks.

Clott shrugs.

'This bust-up with Figg is big,' he sighs. 'I don't think

a bit of tree climbing is going to change Tum's mind anytime soon.'

'It's sooo much more than climbing!' you argue, pointing out how Bin Weevils need to get up to the yellow fly nests in the top branches of Tink's Tree and then use Scent Flowers to attract the insects back down towards the roots.

After another excruciating pause, Tink utters the words that always fill you with dread.

'I've got another idea.'

Clott claps his hands together in glee. He ignores your frantic head shaking and demands to hear Tink's plan.

'Flem Manor's just across the water,' announces Tink. 'Why don't we pay a visit to Scribbles?'

'Why would we want to do that?' you ask. If this scheme is any good, you make a silent promise to eat Clott's hat.

Tink points out that Scribbles is the editor of *Weevil Weekly*, the magazine that published Figg's angry letter about Tum.

'That magazine seems to have a Mulch-load of power round here,' continues Tink. 'Everybody's reading it! We need to persuade Scribbles to let us write an article to set the record straight. We could even put in an interview with Gam saying that every major birthday celebration needs two big birthday cakes rather than one! Figg and Tum would lap that kind of publicity up!'

You ask Clott to pass you his hat and a knife and fork. Tink's plan is bold, bonkers and . . . quite brilliant! Figg and Tum both dream of being famous – a glowing write-up in the Bin's fave magazine could be their first step towards celebrity! You are sure they'd stop their feud and concentrate on making two party-perfect cakes.

You take a deep breath. Do you betray your better judgement and go with Tink's new suggestion, or stick to your gut instincts?

Tink and Clott flash you their goofiest grins. When it comes to brainwaves, they certainly don't have the best track record. You think back to the disastrous Pea Pod Canoe business on Tycoon Island. Too many things have gone wrong too many times for these amigos!

If you opt to play it safe and push on to Tink's Tree, go to page 7.
If you decide to find Scribbles, go to page 46.

You sink down to your knees beside Slam.

'We've got a teensy-weensy problem,' you explain, before spilling out the entire, sorry story. Slam's headphones slip in surprise.

Tink and Clott listen too, forgetting that they've heard it all before! Within minutes, the chums are crying big, salty tears.

'How are we going to win Tum and Figg round?' you ask, wondering if now might be a good time to emigrate to a brand new Bin.

Slam grins, then hands you a roll of tape and some flowery paper.

'Tum and Figg are ladies,' she begins. 'And ladies love presents . . .'

'So?' asks Clott.

You leap to your feet. 'So we soften them up with a present!'

You dive into your backpack and pull out the two scrumptious ingredients that Gam gave you at the start of the mission.

'Tum would love the crushed beetle meringue and Figg will go nuts for the pot of chocolate sludge,' you cry. 'Come on, Bin Weevils. Let's get wrapping!'

You look at your watch. There should just be time to deliver the gifts before the party countdown begins. Slam has cleverly labelled the goodies so that Figg and Tum will each think the surprise is a peace offering from the other one. Genius!

Your mission buddies give you a high five. You don't know quite how you did it, but somehow you

managed to pull off Gam's mission impossible.
  Congratulations!

The End

You, Tink and Clott scramble out of Scribbles' office. You've got thirty minutes to find the scoop of the century!

As you screech up the path to Flum's Fountain, a smart Bin Tycoon raises his top hat to you. It's Dosh, the most minted Bin Weevil in the Binscape! Dosh is rolling in Mulch, literally. He gets up to his feet and dusts himself down.

'This stack of Mulch got creased in the washing machine,' he explains. 'Just trying to flatten it out before Gam's birthday. Thought I'd give the old boy a million Mulch to spend as a gift from the Dosh family.'

Suddenly a light bulb pops in your head.

'Perhaps you'd let us write about you in a news story for *Weevil Weekly*?' you suggest.

Dosh agrees. You ask all the right questions, catching everything on tape. Dosh asks if you've got everything you need.

'It's great, but we need something more exclusive for the headline story.' You pretend to think for a minute. 'How about we write a story about you sponsoring Tum and Figg to create a surprise cake for the birthday party?'

'Tum and Figg are both making rival cakes,' says Tink. 'If you commissioned them to put the two together, the creation would be knock-out!'

'We must speak to Figg and Tum immediately!' shouts Dosh.

You, Tink and Clott give each other a high five. Once your little piece hits the headlines, Gam's boisterous bakers are bound to call a truce! Dosh will be delighted and the residents of the Bin will have a colossal cake to share. Awesome work, Bin Weevils!

The End

It's the beginning of a very nervous wait. Have you done the right thing? What will Figg say when she sees Tum? What will Tum say when she sees Figg? You heart is thumping, but as a loyal member of the Secret Weevil Service, you have to give it a go.

'Why are we doing this again?' asks Tink. 'Sounds worse than one of my Mulch-making schemes.'

You explain your theory that when Figg sees Tum's collapsed cake, she'll feel sorry for her rival and call all this silliness off.

'Either that or it'll make things a hundred times worse,' adds Clott helpfully.

You are just about to give him a jab in the ribs when the door of the Party Box swings open. Sunbeams suddenly flood in. You can just make out a figure silhouetted in the light. You leap to your feet. It must be Figg!

'What's going on 'ere then?' grunts a voice. 'Party started without me?'

Rott steps into the Party Box. The boss of the dump can sniff out a shindig from the other side of the Binscape! He rubs the belly sticking out through his grotty string vest.

'You're a day early,' you sigh.

You grab a glass of Slime Juice from the bar and press it into Rott's dirty mitts. The Bin Weevil shuffles off to the other side of the dance floor as the door swings open again.

'Now what's this all about?' asks Figg. 'I'm busy in the cafe. Did my Doughnut Tower get delivered safely . . . aaahhhH!'

Figg is in such a rush to strut into the room she slips in the melted Chocolate Sludge Cake! You dive across the floor to catch her, but it's too late. She's coated in messy brown goo from the top of her orange hat right down to the hem of her pinny.

You help the flustered waitress to her feet, giving her a minute to wipe the melted mud off her face.

Figg's eyes narrow. She's spotted someone looming over your shoulder.

'Tum!'

If Figg blames Tum for her sludge-stained uniform, go to page 58.
If she takes pity on Tum's predicament, go to page 75.

'Tink!' you shout. 'Gam hasn't got the energy to start training Bin Pets – he's really old!'

The soppy Bin Weevil peers mournfully inside. You slowly unclasp his fingers from the window frame and drag him away.

'But they're soooo cute!' he begs, flashing you his best puppy-weevil eyes. 'We've just got to have one!'

'Now don't be so silly,' argues Clott, shoving Tink over to look in himself. 'Oh! Oh, they are rather lovely, aren't they? Shall we then? Shall we? SHALL WE?'

You shake your head in despair. It's time to give your friends the 'Bin Pets are for life' chat. After you've listed all the reasons why Gam wouldn't appreciate his own little pocket pal, you drag the jelly-brained duo over to Zing's counter.

'Zowie!' cries Zing. 'Sooo wonderful to see you all!'

You grin at Tink and Clott. Zing always gives you a zesty welcome! As usual the counter in front of her is packed with flashing lights, disco balls and a stack of cool, futuristic stuff.

'We're after a present for Gam's birthday,' explains Clott.

'Nothing boring,' adds Tink, still sulking about the Bin Pets.

'Zap that!' agrees Zing, skipping over to a massive display stand. 'Come and check out my latest delivery.'

Zing shows you the latest in high-tech Bin gear. There is a plinky plonk piano that plays by itself, a bubble-gum dispenser with added chew, and an LED display to put your name up in lights. All totally now and totally cool. Just not totally Gam.

You go through shelf after shelf, searching for inspiration. Zing digs out candyfloss machines, talking money boxes and remote-control cars. Nothing seems quite right.

'Is there anything else?' you beg. 'Anything at all!'

43

A rare frown flashes across Zing's face.

'Only this,' she admits, pulling a box out from underneath the counter. She opens up the lid. There is a pair of record decks inside, but Zing explains that they're faulty. 'The turntables are supposed to play any tune you ask for,' she explains, 'but there's something wrong with the computer chip. Haven't been able to play a sound! Needs to be packed up and sent back to the makers.'

'Good idea,' agrees Clott. 'What a load of rubbish!'

'No it isn't!' you shout.

Tink and Clott wrinkle their noses. Not for the first time this week, they are starting to wonder if you have gone stark, staring mad.

'Gam is not going to want a broken record deck as a birthday present,' argues Tink.

'I couldn't agree with you more,' you reply, 'but I still want to buy it. How much, Zing?'

'A thousand Mulch,' she beams. 'Half price.'

It takes all of your combined weevily power for you, Tink and Clott to drag the package to Slam's Party Box. You unpack the decks and set them on the top table. Disco dude Fling is already there, fixing up lights for Gam's big birthday bash.

'What are those doing here?' he calls. 'I've got the tunes sorted!'

'I know,' you reply in a chipper voice. 'This isn't a music machine.'

Tink and Clott exchange confused stares.

'What is it then?' they demand.

You make an excited little cough.

'This is a Rotating Double Birthday Cake Display Stand!' you announce with enormous pride. 'Just the thing to show off Figg *and* Tum's cookery creations!'

Your pals are totally impressed – you might just have cracked the battle of the cakes!

When you present your idea to the Binscape's bakers, the novel new invention is an overwhelming hit. Tum and Figg grudgingly accept double-billing in the cake stakes – Gam is chuffed to bits when he hears the news.

'Sterling work, Bin Weevils!' he says, slapping you each on the back.

You, Tink and Clott leave SWS HQ with broad smiles plastered across your faces. Not only is it party time, you've still got 1,000 Mulch left to spend!

The End

Cre-eakk!

'I must be mad,' you sigh, pushing open the giant green doors of Flem Manor. Tink and Clott scuttle in behind you, sniggering with excitement.

'Don't worry,' Clott assures you, 'Tink's plans are always genius!'

You know very well that Tink's plans are *never* genius, but it's too late now. Scribbles is calling you into his office!

The editor of *Weevil Weekly* is sat at his desk, surrounded by mounds of scrunched-up balls of paper. The bins are full to overflowing with torn sheets covered in crossed-out notes, doodles and scrawls.

'What's the scoop?' cries Scribbles, leaping out of his chair. 'Got any news for me?'

'We've come about Figg's letter in the magazine,' you explain. 'Tum's very upset.'

Scribbles nods and says he's sorry. He thought Figg's note was a bit harsh, but you can't stop free speech in the Bin!

'That's yesterday's news anyway,' he frowns, sinking back into his chair. 'The next issue of *Weevil Weekly* goes to press today and I haven't got a headline story! If I don't find one soon, this magazine's history!'

Clott's eyes fill with tears.

'What are we gonna do?' he wails. 'We can't have an issue of *Weevil Weekly* with nothing in it!'

Tink nudges his pal in the ribs. 'We have got something to go in it, Clott,' he whispers. '*Remember*?'

Scribbles grabs a notepad and rushes round to the other side of the desk. He pulls a pencil out from under his antennae and gets ready to hear what we've got to say.

'We want to publish a piece setting the record straight about Tum and Figg's feud,' you say. 'If we don't do it soon, Gam's birthday party is going to turn into a sponge-hurling disaster!'

'That's interesting,' Scribbles agrees. 'Tell me more.'

You, Tink and Clott all start talking at once. You want to get everything in – how Tum and Figg are actually *both* the best bakers in the Bin, but if they don't start working together Gam's celebration feast will crumble into a giant bun fight! You explain that Figg's letter wasn't really true, making Tum so hopping mad she decided to buy up all the candles in town. When you've finished dishing, Scribbles has a funny look in his eye.

'I can see the headline now,' he announces, looking off into the middle distance. You, Tink and Clott rush round behind him to share the view. '"WARRING BIN WEEVILS BIN BIRTHDAY BASH!" Roll the presses!'

'No! That's not it at all!' gulps Clott, his bottom lip starting to tremble. 'If you print that it will just make everything worse!'

Scribbles is already one step ahead of you. He rushes over to his computer and starts bashing the keys like a Bin Weevil possessed.

'You can't stand in the way of the facts,' he tells you. 'Hold the front page!'

Agent Tink and Agent Clott both shoot you a pleading look. This mission has just hit a major new setback!

'What do we do now?'

If you decide to try to persuade Scribbles to rethink the story, go to page 15.
If you reckon you'll have more luck publishing your own magazine, go to page 74.

47

You, Tink and Clott take turns wheeling the Scent Flower back through the dirty paths and passageways of the Bin. All along the way, envious Bin Weevils wander over to admire its glossy petals and sniff its unique stink.

'Think of the flies this beauty will attract,' grins Clott. 'What a scent!'

When you arrive at Tum's Diner, you take a moment to agree your plan of action.

'I'll do the talking,' you tell Tink and Clott. 'You enjoy the smell.'

Tink takes a deep breath.

'You got it!'

You push the wheelbarrow straight through the restaurant and into the kitchen out the back. Inside you find Tum standing on a stepladder, squeezing melting mud on to a giant, triple-tiered Chocolate Sludge birthday cake. She is concentrating so hard on her squelchy icing, she doesn't even look up.

'Not now, Slum!' she shrieks. 'If the customers don't like it, give 'em a refund.'

You cough politely to gain her attention.

Nothing.

You cough again a little louder, clearing your throat with a phlegmy 'a-hem'.

Nothing again.

You are about to hack all over the kitchen when Tink shouts 'Oi!' at the top of his voice. Tum gets down from her stepladder.

'What are you doing in my . . .' she begins, before trailing off in surprise. Tum tiptoes up to your Scent Flower and takes a big, deep breath.

'What a heavenly smell!' she coos.

'We grew it,' Clott explains proudly.

'We wanted to show you what teamwork could do,' you add. 'We were hoping it might persuade you to join forces with Figg.'

'Never mind that,' scoffs Tum, dismissing you with a wave of her hand. 'This gorgeous pong is just what I need to give my cake the flavour it's lacking! Can I have it?'

You break into a broad, toothy grin. The hot-headed chef can of course have your Scent Flower, at a very special price. You explain that Tum has to agree to make things up with Figg before you can even consider handing the flower over.

Tum agrees at once. For the sake of a perfect cake, she swallows her pride and puts in a call to Figg's Cafe. The pair feel soooo much better once they're talking again, making a pact to bake two complementary creations for the birthday feast.

'Come on, lads!' you grin to Tink and Clott. 'Time to report back to Castle Gam.' Mission accomplished!

The End

You wave goodbye to Bunty, taking a seat beneath Dosh's Mulch-encrusted statue. Time is ticking by, but your mission hardly seems to have got off the ground! You sit for a while staring into the plaza, wondering what to do next.

'While we're here, I'd better stick my head into Clott's Garden Plots,' says Clott. 'Just in case I've had any customers. Back in a mo!'

Clott's shop sells garden extensions – Bin Weevils can expand their gardens to up to four times their original size. He doesn't sell them very often, however, because he's too busy swanning round the Binscape with Tink! You watch your pal unlock the shop and wander inside.

While you wait for Clott, you decide to have a brainstorming session. Tink throws ideas at you thick and fast, but as usual he's forgotten to engage his brain before speaking. You are just explaining why it would never work to ask the chefs to sort out their differences with a dance-off at Fling's nightclub, when Clott blunders out of the Garden Plot shop so fast he nearly floors Dosh's statue!

'How's business?' you ask. 'Did you make any sales?'

Clott nods his head. 'Just the one.'

He lifts up his top hat to reveal wads and wads of Mulch! You listen open-mouthed as Clott explains that a Bin Tycoon has bought a super-deluxe garden extension that very morning. As the shop was empty, the honest Bin Weevil left the cash on the counter.

'We are rolling in wonga!' he jabbers.

You and Tink can hardly believe your luck. After you've finished cheering, dancing and rolling in banknotes, Clott is ready to make his first purchase.

'We can do a lot of good with this Mulch,' he decides. 'Follow me.'

If Clott decides to take you to Rum's Airport, go to page 10.
If the lucky Bin Weevil directs you to Rigg's Movie Multiplex instead, go to page 34.

'Righto!' claps Clott. 'Let's go and show Tum how clever we've been!'

'She's going to be knocked out,' sniggers Tink. 'I wonder what the seed will grow into?'

You nod proudly, turning the little acorn over and over in your palm. There are stories across the Bin that these rare seeds can grow into mighty Scent Flowers, Step Mushrooms or maybe even another Tink's Tree.

'We could even plant it in her garden,' you suggest. 'The Garden Inspector would be super-impressed!'

Once Tum sees the value of teamwork, you are sure that she'll be knocking on Figg's door with an irresistible plan for a brand new birthday cake, manufactured by T and F Associates.

'And when Figg sees Tum's plant, I bet she'll want one too,' Clott adds happily.

Ulch. You hadn't thought of that.

'Back up the tree, fellas,' you order. 'We need to get those flies swarming again. If Figg sees that she's been left out of this little seed-fest she will *not* be impressed!'

Tink and Clott sigh wearily, but nod their heads. To make the task a little sweeter, you dig the beaker of crushed beetle meringue out of your backpack and share it out. One delicious snack later and the three of you are back to work.

If you fancy earning two seeds today, go to page 33!

'Psst!' you hiss.

Fink suddenly leaps out from behind a column, giving Tum a terrible fright.

'Will you go and find Slum?' you urge. 'He could be a Bin Weevil on the edge right now.'

Fink races out of the Party Box, while you crouch down next to Tum. Her cake can't be saved – you're going to have to talk your way out of this one.

'Don't cry,' you say, handing her a tissue. 'It's not the end of the world if Gam doesn't have a Chocolate Sludge Cake for his birthday.'

Tum throws her hands in the air and wails. You try a different tack.

'I heard that he's not got a sweet tooth anyway. In fact I don't think he's got any teeth at all,' you ramble. 'I'd say that canapés would be more up his street. What about those lovely Bin Burgers you make?'

'They are rather famous across the Bin,' Tum concedes.

To your delight, Tum takes the idea and runs with it. She quickly dismisses the birthday cake project as passé, clearing the way for Figg! Tum is so set on making a scene-stealing selection of canapés, she even agrees to give her haul of birthday candles back.

A few minutes later Fink marches in with Slum.

'What have I done now?' yelps Tum's helper. 'I didn't mean to drop the cake!'

Tum sweeps Slum into tight hug.

'Come on,' she beams, 'there's work to do!'

The End

You give Dosh a friendly wave.

'Would love to chat, but I've got a very important delivery to oversee,' you explain.

You push the trolley across the vast dance floor that Slam has set up. Spotlights shine and glitter above the rows of chairs and tables. It's going to be quite a party!

'Check out Fling's moves!' you cry, watching the Bin's most famous disco dude spin underneath the disco ball.

Fling lifts his super-cool shades and strikes a pose.

'Cake needs to go over there, dude!'

You trundle the trolley into position in between the drinks counter and the present table.

'Hi!'

Slam looks up at you. The hostess is kneeling behind the table, surrounded by a pile of gift-wrap, tape and scissors. She really is the ultimate wrapper.

'Just getting the last of Gam's presents ready,' she smiles. 'Not long to go now.'

'That's right,' nods Tink. 'Shame we haven't sorted out the cake sitch. There's gonna be one heck of a dust-up!'

Tink is right. Unless you come up with something pronto, the whole mission is going to be a failure! You need to stay calm and think on your feet.

54

If you decide to ask Fling for some creative inspiration, go to page 26.

If you think you've got more hope getting help by picking Slam's Bin brain, go to page 38.

'Well,' presses Nab. 'What's your call?'

'If you can guarantee the liquidizer *and* the microwave, I'll accept the deal,' you say bravely.

Nab whistles through his teeth.

'That microwave could earn me a lot of Mulch.'

Nab pretends to think about it. A nervy silence falls over the Haggle Hut.

'I'd love to help you,' he sneers, 'but business is business!'

Suddenly Tum appears in the Hut doorway!

'Perhaps this will change your mind,' she barks, slapping a fistful of Mulch on the table. 'I want everything back, including my rotten egg timer.'

'Done!' Nab cries. 'Help yerselves!'

You don't hang around to ask questions. You and Tum load yourselves up with crocks, pots and kitchen gizmos before Nab changes his mind. It's not till you're back at the diner enjoying one of Slum's extra-special Double Bin Burgers that Tum explains her well-timed guest appearance.

'When I heard what you and the Bin Boys were willing to do to make Gam's bash work out, I felt more than a little bit silly,' she sniffs. 'I was so ashamed I phoned Figg and asked her to make the birthday cake.'

You, Tink and Clott breathe a deep sight of relief. Not only is the party back on, you've earned yourselves an all-you-can-eat pass at one of the scrummiest eateries in town. Bring on the Bin Burgers!

The End

56

You can hardly hear yourself think. Hem and Ink are both bombarding you with ideas for the headline story of *Weevil Weekly*, shouting at the top of their very loud voices.

'This is getting us nowhere!' you howl.

Tink and Clott jump on Snappy's counter. It's time to call for order, Bin Weevil-style.

'STOOOOPPPPPPPP!!'

Hem and Ink blink in surprise.

'I'm sorry,' you sigh, 'but I don't think either of you have got a headline for me that's going to make it into Gam's birthday issue.'

'I am not appreciated, *again*!' sniffs Ink. He closes his book with a dusty snap and flounces out of the Photo Shop.

Hem is about to turn on her fashionable heels too, when she spies her hat in the mirror.

'I may not be a great writer,' she shrugs, 'but there is something else I can do. Why don't I present Figg and Tum with a stunning couture hat each, as a thank you for Gam's birthday feast? You could take our photos for the front cover of the magazine!'

The rest is history. Tum and Figg were so delighted with their new headgear, they put their differences aside and posed together for the front cover of *Weevil Weekly*. Hem got the publicity she craved and a Binload of new customers. Gam got two delish birthday cakes and the best birthday feast in Bin history. Well done, Agent, mission accomplished!

The End

Tum is so shocked she stops crying.

'Look what you've done to my dress!' shrieks Figg, smearing the Chocolate Sludge off her order pad.

'It's not my fault my cake got splatted!' bellows the chef, scrunching up a hankie and hurling it at Tink.

Clott gives you an 'I-told-you-so' look.

You step in between the ladies, begging for them both to calm down. Neither one is listening. Instead the yelling gets louder and louder and louder.

'How could you swipe all those candles?' snaps Figg. 'You should stand aside and let me make the cake. Everyone loves my Dirt Doughnuts!'

Tum folds her hands over her chest, retorting that if someone hadn't written a nasty letter to *Weevil Weekly*, she might have been persuaded to share them out.

You gulp. Could this mission really be doomed to end in utter failure?

'Fink,' you whisper. 'Blow your whistle!'

PppeeeeeeeeEEEEPPP!

For just a moment, Figg and Tum stop shouting. This is your last chance.

'Ladies,' you beg. 'Please see reason . . . for Gam's sake. He might be old, but he's still a superhero. Would you like to be personally responsible for spoiling his birthday?'

Tum and Figg shake their heads.

'Let's look at the facts,' you continue. 'Figg has a mouth-watering stack of Dirt Doughnuts, Tum has a squashed (but exceedingly delicious) Chocolate Sludge Cake with extra melted mud and one hundred candles. There must be a way we  can put all that together to make something really knock-out!'

The bakers look sheepish and then . . . inspired!

Figg takes a lick of the chocolate sponge dripping down her frock.

'Mmmm . . . I guess this *could* make a nice topping for my Doughnut Tower,' she admits.

Tum's face brightens. From that very small beginning, a great partnership is formed.

Tink grabs you and Clott by the collar, then retreats towards the door.

'We'll leave you chefs to work your magic,' he grins. 'Bet it's going to be AMAZING!'

And it is. On the stroke of midnight the next day, Tum and Figg wheel out the most spectacular Chocolate Dirt Doughnut Sludge Tower the Bin has ever seen! Gam is delighted. Bin Weevils are still feasting on the giant cake stack a week later!

When the party is in full swing, Gam calls you to his chair.

'That was a tough assignment,' he says, 'but you didn't let me down. Good work, Agents!'

The End

'Bin Pets aren't cheap,' you say dubiously. 'What if Gam doesn't want the trouble of training it?'

Tink and Clott aren't listening. They've already walked in the door. You reluctantly follow the duo inside.

'Let's get a red one!' begs Clott.

'Grey's cute, too,' adds Tink. 'We could call it "Tinky". Please. Per-lease!'

You try to resist, but then you catch the eye of an adorable little fella with a green body and bright orange legs. Before you know it you're walking out of the shop with the critter tucked under your arm, along with a bowl, basket and a large box of Pet Mulch!

'How did that just happen?' you wonder, bouncing the little chap on your knee. You decide to call him 'Lucky'.

'Let's take Lucky back to my nest,' suggests Clott. 'He can stay with me until Gam's party! I'm going to teach him to juggle.'

Tink reaches forward and lifts the Bin Pet out of your arms.

'Nah! I want Lucky to stay with me,' he argues, placing a slurpy kiss on the little guy's head.

Tink and Clott wander out of the Shopping Mall, passing the Bin Pet between them. Poor Lucky squeaks helplessly, not liking the game of Binny-in-the-Middle! By the time you get to Flum's Fountain, you're ready to ask for a refund!

'What kind of lesson do you think this is teaching Lucky?' you scold Tink and Clott. 'Stop snatching and start sharing!'

Will Tink and Clott play nicely with Gam's birthday pet? The answer's on page 5!

61

You clamber out of a large brass pipe and take a look around. You're standing on the top of a towering skyscraper. A gold-plated chopper gleams on the helipad in front of you. Swanky restaurants and apartment blocks flash against the skyline. There's only one place in the Bin you can be – Tycoon Island!

A smart Bin Weevil dressed in pink scampers towards Tycoon Plaza. You immediately recognize your pal Bunty. Bunty is a personal assistant in the Tycoon Shop, the most exclusive store in town. She prides herself on knowing all the latest goss – if it's been done, said or even thought, Bunty will know it first!

'Pssst!' Tink whispers in your ear. 'Perhaps she's got the inside story on Gam's birthday?'

'Hello, Bunty,' you smile. 'Got a minute?'

'Hi, darlinks!' she coos. 'I should really be getting along to work, but I've always got time for my friends.'

Tink tries to lean casually against the Slime Pool pipe, but misses and lands on the floor. He picks himself up again, wincing at the knock.

'So, Bunty!' he grins awkwardly. 'What's new?'

Bunty takes a deep breath.

'Well . . .'

You wish you had never asked. Bunty can talk the hind-legs off the back of a Bin Weevil! She's dished the dirt on every resident in the Bin, before moving on to their friends, neighbours and second cousins twice removed. You try to get a word in edgeways, but it's impossible. Bunty doesn't even stop for breath! Two hours later, the conversation finally turns to Tum and Figg's fight.

'Now, *that*!' she cries. 'I have got sooooo much to tell you about that. I suppose you read Figg's dreadful letter in *Weevil Weekly*?'

Before Bunty can continue, Clott stops her in her tracks.

'Wibble.'

'Pardon?' asks Bunty. 'What did he just say?'

Tink puts his arm round Clott and nods his head in an understanding way.

'I believe he just said "wibble".'

'Why the drainpipes would he say that?' wonders Bunty.

You and Tink know exactly why. Clott is saying what he always says when he spots the one Bin Weevil that he's just dying to impress – Posh!

If you want to stay and hear if Bunty has a new angle on the whole Figg and Tum sitch, go to page 20.
If you decide to shake off Bunty and catch up with Posh, go to page 81.

You follow Posh down to the Slime Pool, the coolest hangout in the Bin. You'd totally forgotten how awesome it is! Laughing Tycoons whizz down the water slide, landing at the bottom in a squelchy pool of slime. The rest of the jet set are chillaxing to tropical grooves outside the Smoothie Shack.

'Four of my usual please, barman!' trills Posh.

Clott is still too awestruck to speak when she hands each of you a scrummy Peach on the Beach smoothie, insisting that this is her treat.

You take a big glug and lick your lips.

'You know what this needs?' you say. 'A bit of crunch.'

You pull Figg's Dirt Doughnut out of your pocket and sprinkle some into your smoothie. It tastes awesome. Excited, you pull the pot of Chocolate Sludge out of your rucksack and add some of that, too. It's a taste bud-exploding flavour sensation!

'I say,' gushes Posh. 'You've invented a brand new recipe.'

You nod proudly.

'Imagine a Peach on the Beach birthday cake flavoured with Tum's Chocolate Sludge and Figg's Dirt Doughnuts!'

'It'd be fruity fantastic!' Tink bellows, his jaw dropping. 'We gotta tell Tum and Figg!'

You give yourself a slap on the back. You've found the perfect solution to Gam's birthday mission! Clott is so thrilled, even he finds the courage to speak.

'Wibble.'

The End

Tink starts nodding. Nab rubs his hands greedily.

'Let's take a chance,' you smile, giving your pal's waistcoat a hard tug. 'I'm feeling lucky. How about we strike *you* a deal?'

'What have you got in mind?'

Nab leans in further. It's your one and only chance to set the stakes high!

'Cup number one gives us all of Tum's stuff, cup number two gives us nothing,' you say, meeting the Bin Weevil's stare. 'But cup number three gives us all the gear *and* 2,000 Mulch.'

There's a sharp intake of breath from Clott. Tink has passed out on the floor.

Nab thinks it over for a moment, then nods, unable to resist the gamble. He just loves to play this game. He marks the inside of the cups ONE, TWO and THREE, then sets them back down.

Your heart thumps as he begins to switch the cups back and forth. Nab's gold tooth glints in the light as he moves them faster and faster.

'OK,' he says at last. 'Pick a cup.'

You point to the middle cup.

Nab's face freezes as he turns it over. You can hardly bear to look.

The next thing you hear is the rusty ring of the Haggle Hut cash register.

'Take your rotten stuff and get outta here!' he yells, thrusting 2,000 juicy Mulch into your mitts.

Tink and Clott hurdle the counter, hooting with delight as they load up with pots and pans. You did it. By some sheer weevily fluke, you actually managed to trick a trickster!

After Slum has been reunited with his beloved liquidizer and the rest of the kitchen gear, it's time for stage two of your mission. Tum and Figg are still at war *and* you've still got a birthday cake to sort out.

You decide to take a stroll to the Shopping Mall. You haven't got a plan, but you do have 2,000 Mulch burning a hole in your pocket!

'Maybe we can buy Gam's birthday present,' suggests Clott, gazing longingly at the shiny shop windows. 'Let's see what Zing's got in stock to show us!'

You are just about to follow Clott to Zing's counter when you notice that Tink has disappeared into the crowds of shoppers. You elbow your way through the crowds, trying to spot him.

'There he is!' you cry at last.

Tink is stood on tiptoes with his nose pressed against a store window.

'Where's the Mulch?' he demands. 'I wanna buy Gam a Bin Pet!'

If you think Tink's gone potty, go to page 43.
If you can imagine Gam with his very own Bin Pet, go to page 61.

'What's your idea, Ink?' you ask, leaving Hem to sulk in the corner. 'I've got to find something that will stop Tum and Figg's fight from spoiling Gam's big day!'

Ink suggests writing a poem. Not just any poem, but a special poem from Figg's point of view, that says sorry to Tum and makes amends.

Tink and Clott look puzzled. You're fairly puzzled yourself.

'But that would be lying, wouldn't it?' says Tink.

'Yeah,' agrees Clott, 'cos Figg doesn't want to say sorry to Tum.'

Ink has got a devilish look in his eye.

'I am an artiste! It would be a work of fiction,' he announces grandly to the room, before adding very quietly, 'that is "inspired", shall we say, by real-life events.'

'Dangerous move, boys,' humphs Hem.

It *is* dangerous, but it's got to be worth a try. What other option do you have? The last thing that Scribbles will want to read about is an article on Hem's new range of tinfoil tiaras. A sensational letter from 'Figg' however, might just get Tum back on side!

'Get writing, Ink!' you say. 'We've got to get this piece to Flem Manor, like, yesterday!'

Ink bows dramatically.

'I start NOW!' he cries. 'I shall want paying, of course.'

You rummage around in your pockets, Tink checks his waistcoat and Clott looks under his hat. You've only got a handful of Mulch between you and there's still Gam's present to buy! When you check the zips of your backpack one last time, you spot the pot of chocolate sludge and the beaker of crushed beetle meringue that Gam gave you at the start of the mission.

'Will this do?' you ask, a pleading look in your eye.

Ink dips a finger in the chocolate sludge pot, then gives it a thoughtful lick.

'My favourite!' he declares. 'Now prepare to watch a master do his work . . .'

You, Tink and Clott wait with bated breath, but Ink does not fail you. His 'Sonnet From A Sorry Chef' is a masterpiece! After a heart-stopping rush to Scribbles' office, the editor agrees to ditch the 'WARRING BIN WEEVILS' headline and run Ink's poem instead.

As soon as the first issue is hot off the press, you take it over to Tum's Diner. Tum melts the minute she reads the headline.

'Oh, poor Figg,' she sobs. 'Perhaps I have been too hasty.'

Now it is time for the most daring part of your plan. Somehow you manage to persuade Tum not to mention the poem to Figg, in order to protect her feelings. Tink and Clott have just spent a nail-biting afternoon making sure she doesn't read the late edition of *Weevil Weekly*!

When Tum arrives at Figg's Cafe with a parcel of birthday candles for her rival, she is, of course, the soul of discretion. Figg isn't sure why she has arrived to make amends, but she is very pleased. Together the friends forge a plan to make a brand new birthday cake, combining all of their considerable pastry skills. There's going to be Dirt

Doughnuts, crushed beetle meringue and oodles of extra sludge.

Your job is done. Bring on Gam's party!

The End

'Whoa, Figg,' you plead. 'It was just a suggestion! You're the top chef round here. When it comes to Dirt Doughnuts, what you say goes.'

'That's all right then,' sniffs the cafe owner. 'If you'll excuse me I've got to start building my Doughnut Tower.'

Tink and Clott sigh with relief. You've managed to keep yourself in Figg's good books for now, but only just.

You watch Figg expertly pile her doughnuts on to a trolley. The finished pyramid looks utterly scrummy! You're tempted to sample one more teensy-weensy Doughnut, but if the tower topples you daren't face the consequences! Figg gets ready to push her birthday creation over to Slam's Party Box.

'Can we have some service out here!' yells a voice from out front.

Tink disappears out of the kitchen, then scurries back in again.

'You've got customers waiting,' he shrugs, before adding, 'And lots of 'em!'

Figg doesn't know what to do. She can't run the cafe *and* deliver the cake at the same time. You give Agents Tink and Clott a knowing wink – this sounds like the perfect opportunity for you to progress Operation Party Cake!

'We'll deliver the Doughnuts,' you offer, taking hold of the trolley.

Figg pulls the trolley back towards her, too nervous to let go of the delicious cakes. Tink and Clott's reputation as bunglers and bodgers isn't helping much either.

'Look at the time,' you press. 'The Doughnuts will melt if they stand for too long in this steamy kitchen.'

Figg glares at Tink and Clott, then reluctantly agrees.

After threatening you each with a lifetime ban from her cafe if a single Doughnut gets dropped, eaten or damaged, she ushers you out of the kitchen.

You and your friends take turns trundling the trolley along the dusty path that leads to Slam's Party Box. You still aren't sure how helping Figg is going to sort her row with Tum, but you're bound to think of something.

A few moments later, Clott spots someone striding towards you. It's Fink, the Binscape's self-appointed super-sleuth! The nosy Bin Weevil is patrolling the grounds of Flem Manor, making sure that no crimes are being committed on the eve of Gam's party.

'What's going on 'ere, then?' asks Fink, eyeing the trolley suspiciously. He pulls out a notebook and starts taking down your particulars.

'Maybe he can help us?' whispers Clott. 'Let's talk to him.'

71

Tink violently shakes his head, remembering 'The Case of The Missing Cereal'. It took Fink three and a half weeks just to work out that Tink had eaten the primary evidence for breakfast!

'Fink's investigations take for-e-v-e-r,' he argues. 'We need to get to the Party Box!'

If you decide to ask Fink for help, go to page 31.
If you decide to put your heads down and carry on,
    go to page 82.

'Come on, lads!' you cheer. 'I bet you're brilliant at the Daily Brain Strain! Let's look in at Lab's Lab.'

Tink and Clott wince at each other, but dutifully trail after you. Somehow you manage to get the Dirt Doughnut Tower across the water without toppling it into the murky depths. Before you know it, you're pushing the trolley up the stack of books that lead to Lab's Lab.

'This will do,' you smile, parking the trolley up beside the Mystery Code Machine.

'Shall we stay and guard the Doughnuts?' asks Tink helpfully.

Clott gives an eager nod. 'They'll be much safer with us.'

You won't hear of it – you need your friends' help doing the Daily Brain Strain! You push the trolley out of sight, then head to the chrome pipe that winds into Lab's Lab.

Next to the pipe, you spot a shady Bin Weevil wandering around in circles. When you get closer the figure ducks behind a green spotted mushroom. What is going on?

If you decide to check out the figure lurking behind the mushroom, go to page 19.
If you think it's time to take the Daily Brain Strain challenge, go to page 85.

'Come on, Bin Boys!' you cry. 'It's time to get our fingers inky!'

Scribbles doesn't even look up – he's too busy writing his sensational new story! You, Tink and Clott dash back to your nest to pick up your camera. Back at home, you pull a handful of Mulch out from behind the sofa.

'Go and buy a tape recorder from the Shopping Mall,' you say, handing over the dosh. 'Hurry!'

There isn't a second to waste. You've got to get your magazine out before the next issue of *Weevil Weekly*! If you can flash a glowing article under Tum and Figg's noses pronto they might just bury the hatchet!

The next few hours pass in a blur of roving reporting. It's hard to believe, but by teatime you are actually holding a grimy copy of 'Gam's Happy Birthday Magazine' in your hot sweaty hands. The front cover features two stunning shots of the celebrity cooks in their kitchens, each waving a wooden spoon.

Of course when Tum and Figg see the piece they are thrilled, sticking up copies all over their eateries. Although they don't like to share the spotlight, they can't resist rising to the challenge of both baking Gam a beautiful birthday cake. Tum even agrees to share out the candles!

It's time to sit back and enjoy the party. Your job is done . . . Well, almost. You, Tink and Clott just need to make sure that the cooks don't clap eyes on the latest issue of *Weevil Weekly*. Ever. (Eek!)

The End

74

The sight of Figg wearing her Chocolate Sludge Cake is too much for poor Tum. The battered baker puts her head in her hands and starts to wail even more loudly than before.

Fink can't cope. He creeps quietly towards the door muttering something about having an urgent crime to solve on Mulch Island. You, Tink and Clott prepare yourselves for the ear-bashing that you're sure Figg is about to give you.

'Look on the bright side,' whispers Clott. 'At least there aren't any plates here for her to throw!'

You cover your eyes, wondering quite how you're going to explain to Gam that you managed to ramp the cake feud up to a whole new level.

When you open them again, you're in for a surprise. Figg is crouched on the floor beside Tum, giving her a hug!

'You poor thing,' she soothes. 'I would be beside myself if my cake got squashed. This melted mud topping really is divine!'

Tum blows her nose again. 'I've only got myself to blame, really,' she admits. 'I am sorry I bought all those candles. What a silly thing to do!'

Figg's face blushes into a deep shade of blue. She apologizes for writing such a mean letter to Scribbles. Before you know it, the chefs are making plans to whip up a brand new cake collaboration for Gam's big day!

You, Tink and Clott tiptoe out of the room. Your work here is done! Just as you get to the doorway, the chefs call out your names. You've just given them a cracking new idea . . .

Twenty-four rollercoaster hours later, Gam's party is in full swing. Slam's Party Box is packed with every boogie-ing Bin Weevil in the Bin! At the stroke of midnight, the crowds hush as Tum and Figg wheel the great birthday cake in. Everyone agrees it is a triumph.

'Happy birthday dear Ga-am! Happy birthday to you!'

There is a gasp of surprise as you, Tink and Clott burst out of the centre of the cake. Ta-daaa!

Gam nearly falls off his chair. This truly has been a birthday he'll never forget!

The End

'Figg's our best bet,' you decide, linking arms with Tink and Clott. 'Let's go!'

Tink and Clott dig their feet into the dirt.

'But what if she's still throwing stuff?' argues Tink, shuddering at the very thought. 'All that waiting tables has made Figg a mean plate juggler – she'll be able to lob them at us four at a time!'

'Yeah,' agrees Clott. 'I prefer eating her Club Sandwiches, not *wearing* them!'

You stand firm, explaining that it's either a spot of plate dodging with Figg or an afternoon spent at Tum's Diner listening to Slum sob over his missing liquidizer. The Boys from the Bin both sigh, then follow you down the path that leads to the cafe.

You haven't even reached the bright lights of Rigg's Multiplex when you hear it:

Crash!

Tinkle!

SMASH!

Figg must still be taking it out on the crockery!

Agents Tink and Clott try and duck into Weevil Post, but you're too quick for them. You grab the pair by the collar and march on.

'Be strong, Bin Weevils!' you urge. 'Figg can't have many more plates left!'

It turns out you were right. Now that she's run through the plates, the bugged Bin baker has turned her attention to cups and saucers.

'Take that! And that!' she shrieks, hurling a mug at a Bin Tycoon that dared to praise Tum's Chocolate Sludge Cake. 'My Dirt Doughnuts are in a different league!'

This is not the happy-go-lucky singing waitress you're used to seeing at the cafe – you and your pals need to calm things down a notch! With tempers running this high, flattery is your only option.

'Now hold your Mould Mousses one saucy second,' you cry, elbowing your way through the tables and chairs. '*Everyone* knows that your Doughnuts are something special.'

Figg puts down the teapot, three saucers and a milk jug that she was about to lob next.

'Do you think so?' she asks, her face flushing with pleasure.

You, Tink and Clott nod your heads so hard your antennae nearly drop off. A few more smooth words and Figg is leading you into the kitchen to admire the giant batch of Doughnuts she's cooked up for Gam's birthday.

'Delicious!' you mumble, munching a giant chewy ring.

And you mean it. Tink and Clott would agree if they could, but their mouths are too stuffed full of dough to speak.

'I'm going to build them into a birthday cake tower!' cries Figg. 'There'll be a hundred!'

'Bravo!' you coo, before gently suggesting that the Doughnuts might go nicely with one of Tum's Chocolate Sludge Cakes.

Figg points to the door.

'Tum again?!' she splutters. 'Get outta here!'

If you've got the courage to stay and talk to Figg, go to page 70.
If the time has come for a quick getaway, scuttle off to page 84.

'Who's going in first, then?' asks Tink, shifting nervously from foot to foot.

'Bagsy not me,' pipes up Clott. 'What if Tum hasn't calmed down? We could get ourselves banned from the diner!'

Suddenly Slum comes tumbling through the doors of the restaurant! The unlucky kitchen-hand skids through the dirt, legs and antennae flailing in all directions.

'Stay clear, Bin Weevils,' he warns. 'Tum's just had another Chocolate Sludge Cake tasting. The sponge is still not right!'

You help Slum to his feet and put his chef's hat straight. After thanking him for his advice, you and your pals make a swift exit to the safety of your nest. Talking to Tum right now sounds like a recipe for Trouble topped with a capital T!

'Time to switch to Plan B,' you say, leading Tink and Clott towards the über-stylish fun pad you like to call home.

'I never knew there was a Plan B!' gawps Tink.

'Agent Tink!' you snort, making it clear that he has just made the silliest suggestion ever. '*Of course* there is a Plan B!'

The three of you walk in silence for a while. Tink daydreams about the outrageously yumtastic Bin Scone he's going to have for supper. Clott scratches his head, trying to remember whether he checked his post box before reporting into Castle Gam. And you? You're desperately trying to think up a Plan B.

By the time you get back to your nest, you've cracked it. You lead your friends straight up the garden pipe, with the acorn still tucked under your arm.

'Tum isn't in the mood to talk seeds right now,' you explain. 'So let's plant this little beauty and see what it grows into. It could turn into something *really* impressive!'

Tink reaches for a shovel.

'Let's put it here,' he suggests, digging a patch of grass in between an Indian Cactus and a Cherry Tree. Soon your little seed is planted up and ready to grow.

'La, la, la, la, la, la, laaaaAAAA!!!' trills Clott. 'The Garden Inspector says that it's important to sing opera to your seedlings. If you'd allow me . . .'

You decide not to argue – after just one bar of Clott's warblings a little green shoot pops its head out of the ground!

A few hours later, you and Tink both have your hands clapped over your ears and your jaws wide open. Clott's tuneless singing has managed to raise a stunning Scent Flower!

'Look at that,' marvels Tink. 'It's boot-i-ful!'

And indeed it is. The Scent Flower is a magnificent bloom with a striped trumpet and scarlet petals. It also pongs like nothing you've ever smelt before.

Clott gently unearths the flower and places it in a wheelbarrow.

'Wait till the rest of the Bin get a noseful of this!'

If you decide to take the Scent Flower straight over to Tum's, go to page 48.

If you have other plans for the new arrival, go to page 9.

Sure enough, Posh steps around the corner, swinging her outrageously expensive golden handbag. Her antennae are curled to perfection, her make-up is glossy and her four little feet have been manicured until they shine – Clott is putty in her hands.

'Why hello there!' she coos, holding out a gloved hand.

Clott gives another weak 'Wibble', then faints on the floor. You and Tink yank him up by the armpits and hold him there between you. It is Clott's life goal to impress Posh so much that she will one day speak more than three words to him. This really isn't the coolest of starts.

'We were just having a lovely chat with Bunty,' you smile. 'What are you doing today?'

'I was just off for a glass of something cold at the Smoothie Shack,' replies Posh, whistling for her cute pink Bin Pet, Lady Wawa. 'Care to join me?'

'Sounds mouth-watering,' grins Tink, helping you drag Clott along with you.

'But I haven't finished my story!' pouts Bunty, suddenly realizing that she hasn't spoken for at least thirty seconds.

'Would love to stop and jaw,' you say apologetically, 'but didn't the Tycoon Shop open five minutes ago?'

'Eek! I'm late!' squeaks Bunty, scrambling off to work.

Go to page 64 to share a smoothie with Dosh's well-heeled sister, Posh!

You take Tink's advice. The last thing you need is an extra Bin Weevil to manage – keeping an eye on Tink and Clott is hard enough! You tell Fink that you heard that something's going down at Flum's Fountain, then press on for Slam's Party Box. Fink doesn't need asking twice. The intrepid crime-cracker is skidding off to find the action faster than you can say 'Bin Weevils wiggle their wellies!'

'Come on, Agents,' you shout. 'Let's keep going!'

Pushing a pyramid of Doughnuts is not easy in the Binscape. The grungy paths wobble and wind over mouldy rubbish and rotten leaves. More than once Tink has to do a goalie save to catch a falling snack.

'Are we nearly there yet?' groans Clott, a few hours later. You take a look around you and sigh. You haven't even passed the bright lights of Rigg's Movie Multiplex! At this rate Gam is never going to get a taste of his birthday cake.

In the distance you spot the 8-Ball observatory at the top of Lab's Lab. You remember that you haven't done the Daily Brain Strain yet this morning. It's *the* best way to earn Mulch in the Bin. All you have to do is answer a few simple questions. Easy-peasy!

'If we had a few more Mulch,' you muse, 'perhaps we could pay someone to help us move the Doughnut Tower

to the Party Box. What do you think, Bin Boys?'
Tink and Clott scratch their heads and shrug.

> If you decide to press on to the Party Box,
>   go to page 30.
> If you feel the urge to take a detour to Lab's Lab,
>   go to page 73.

'There's no talking to some Bin Weevils,' you sigh, as Figg finds a broom to sweep you, Tink and Clott out of her kitchen.

'Ouch!' yelps Clott. 'You batted me on the bottom!'

'That'll teach you to mention Tum's name in my cafe!' she yells, shaking the broom at you.

'That's it, guys,' you cry. 'Let's do a runner!'

You scuttle through the grimy streets as fast as your legs can carry you. The three of you keep going until you've scuttled into your nest and locked the doors.

'Now what do we do?' asks Clott, rubbing his sore behind.

Tink gulps. For the first time ever, he doesn't have a crazy, half-cooked plan. You're pretty low on ideas too.

'We can't do *nothing*, so we'll have to do something,' you frown. 'Let's crawl through the Mystery Portal.'

You all flip your heads towards the door with a big blue question mark on the front, knowing that it could lead you anywhere. It's time to do something, even if that something could lead you into the biggest trouble of your life.

Where will the Mystery Portal take you? If you think it will come out on Tycoon Island, go to page 62.
If you think there's a chance you'll pop out in Tum's Diner, go to page 12.

You decide to ignore the stranger and dive into Lab's Lab. You're sure the figure is just a keen mushroom-spotter out on a field trip.

It is dark inside the lab. Strange liquids glisten and drip through test tubes racked up on the walls and spread out over worktops. Giant computers beep their way through mind-melting calculations. You are bending down to examine a specimen under the microscope when Lab breezes in.

'Clott!' he gasps in amazement. 'What a stellar surprise. I would be honoured if you'd do my Daily Brain Strain today – the questions are extra-tricky, just how you like them.'

Despite his intellectual ways, you'd totally forgotten Lab's one weakness – he's the only Bin Weevil in the Bin who thinks that Clott is a genius! Before you can argue, Lab has dragged your pal into the Brain Strain chair.

The results are predictably poor. Clott scores zero! Lab can't make head nor tail of the data. Now you've got no Mulch, a late Doughnut Tower delivery and an unsolved mission on your hands.

'We can't avoid a giant cake clash now,' you sigh, trailing out of the door. 'There's going to be fireworks tomorrow!'

Lab lifts down a test tube bubbling with scarlet liquid. 'Take this,' he insists. 'If you want fireworks, this will explode and pop all evening. It might even make Tum and Figg forget the cake.'

You thank Lab and leave. You haven't solved this SWS assignment, but at least you've found a pretty impressive diversion!

The End

'What a beauty!' you coo, admiring the golden acorn that's glowing in your arms.

Tink and Clott skid to a halt next to you. Before you know it, you're being slung over their shoulders and carried across the wooden bridge that leads to Dosh's Palace.

'No time to chat,' hisses Tink. 'Look behind you!'

You lean round to be confronted by a horde of marauding Bin Weevils, snatching and lunging at the acorn. If you don't get out quick, you're going to lose the ultra-rare seed before you've even got to show it to Tum! You duck underneath the fish-head fountain in front of Dosh's Palace and press yourselves against the wall, hidden by the jet of dirty water.

'Wait here,' you whisper.

You, Tink and Clott try not to sneeze, hiccup or burp as the mob of greedy Bin Weevils gallop past the fountain.

When the coast is clear, you continue on your way. Soon the three of you are standing outside Tum's Diner, ready to show off your prize.

If you decide to go straight in and find Tum, flick back to page 16.

If you think it'll be even better to plant the seed in your garden and show Tum what it grows into, go to page 79.

You slurp another mouthful of your shake, chewing over the options. Tum's a strong Bin Weevil – she isn't going to back down easily! Tink winces as he recounts the time a customer refused to gulp down their Bin Salad at closing time. Tum made sure he left, all right – the Bin Weevil ran out of the shop covered in his mouldy greens, potato peelings and dressing on the side!

'It's hopeless!' sobs Slum, pulling off his gunky chef's hat to beat himself round the head with a wooden spoon. 'If you can't help, who can?'

You pull yourself up to your full height. You didn't join the Secret Weevil Service for nothing! It's time to show Slum the stuff you're made of.

'Who said we couldn't help?' you cry. 'We're going to sort this stinking situation out right now, starting by getting your stuff back! Tink! Clott! Follow me!'

Slum drops his spoon and blinks in surprise.

'Oh, thank you, thank you!' he babbles, following you out of the door. He pulls a screwed-up inventory of kitchen gear out of his apron and stuffs it into the pocket of your backpack. 'This is what I've lost. Tell my liquidizer I love it!'

Before Tink and Clott know it, you're striding confidently in the direction of Gong's Pipenest. You keep going all the way to Nab's Haggle Hut.

'Right then,' you say, standing outside the door. 'We've got to negotiate hard here, Nab strikes a mean bargain. Anybody got any questions?'

Tink and Clott both shake their heads, very fast. They pause for a moment, then begin to nod them very, very slowly.

'Just one thing,' says Clott. 'What are we gonna negotiate *with*?'

You decide to pool your Mulch. Unfortunately you have precisely three Mulch between you.

'Let's not focus on the negative,' you say, scuttling inside. You're sure you'll think of something spectacular sooner or later.

Nab's pink eyes twinkle with delight the instant he sees you.

'Wanna make a deal?' he asks. The shifty shopkeeper shoots a tempting glance at the three upturned cups lined up on the table in front of him.

Tink and Clott start to tremble with the tension.

'Well, yes,' you say, in the most grown-up voice you can muster. 'We want to get back all the kitchen stuff that Tum traded in the other day.'

Nab smirks up at the food-splattered microwave, pots and blenders piled on the shelf behind him.

'Ah, yes!' he beams. 'Finest quality cookware. It's gonna cost you.'

'Well, that's the thing,' you answer. 'We haven't got much Mulch.'

Nab pulls away from the table and sighs.

'Finders keepers, then.'

You, Tink and Clott creep to the corner of the hut and form a tight huddle.

'What do we do now?' hisses Tink.

'I don't know!' you whisper back.

Nab coughs noisily. 'You could use what Mulch you do have to buy *some* of it back, I suppose,' he adds. 'I'm feeling generous today.'

You zip open the backpack and hunt around for Slum's list. Even the liquidizer would be a start! When you rummage around the bag, you spy the pot of chocolate sludge and the beaker of crushed beetle meringue.

'Oh,' you say innocently. 'I have got . . . this!'

You proudly pull the food out of the bag and set it on the counter. A flash of greed passes over Nab's face. You've got him interested.

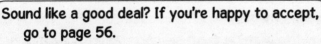

'Hmmm,' he says coolly. 'I'll swap your grub for *half* my stuff.'

Sound like a good deal? If you're happy to accept,
    go to page 56.
If you think the time is right to take a chance,
    go to page 65.

89

'Those bags look snazzy,' you say. 'Very exclusive.'

Dosh couldn't agree with you more. He smirks when he tells you how many hordes of Bin Weevils have already tried to get their hands on one.

You glance over at your cake trolley and an idea starts to form.

'How would you like to have one of Figg's speciality Dirt Doughnuts to go in each of these bags?' you say. 'I've got a limited edition of a hundred.'

Tink starts to blubber, but you elbow him in the ribs. Tink and Clott put their hands over their eyes as you strike a bargain. The Dirt Doughnuts are sold!

'Figg will go mad!' shrieks Clott. 'You can't do that!'

It is an outlandish plan, but it might actually work. In return for the Doughnuts, Dosh agrees to make both Figg and Tum gold star VIPs for the celebrations. Although Figg will be mad at losing out to Tum on the main cake, you're sure that her must-have goodie bags will more than make up for it.

How right can one Bin Weevil be? A day later, your plan has worked without a hitch! Tum's Chocolate Sludge Cake is the main event, but the guests get to take home a little piece of sugary heaven baked by Figg. Everyone is raving about them! The two chefs are even back on speaking terms.

'I never knew you had it in you,' gushes Tink.

Clott gives you a salute. 'Nice working with you, Agent!'

The End

90